W9-CHW-423

Jack Kent's Fables of Aesop

Jack Kent's FABLES OF ÆSOP

CENTRAL PUBLIC SCHOOL LIBRARY

Parents' Magazine Press · New York

Copyright © 1972 by Jack Kent
All rights reserved
Printed in the United States of America
ISBN: Trade 0-8193-0540-5, Library 0-8193-0541-3
Library of Congress Catalog Card Number: 76-181498

CONTENTS

The fables of Aesop have appeared in many forms since they were first collected and set down by him some twenty-five hundred years ago. Socrates himself made poems of some of them, and writers have been embellishing them ever since. Now Jack Kent has developed a fresh variation by means of his artwork. Freely using the V. S. Vernon-Jones version as a point of departure, he has given the stories a new dimension of humor and, while the morals are as true as ever, the reader enjoys a chuckle along with the verities.

THE ASS IN THE LION'S SKIN

An ass found a lion's skin and put it on.
Then he went around scaring people.

Everyone ran when they saw him. They thought he was a lion.

After a while he began to think he was
a lion, too. He opened his mouth to roar,

but all that came out was...

"Oh, it's you, is it?" said
the fox. "You had me fooled
until you opened your mouth."

Sometimes you can get more respect by
keeping your mouth shut.

THE BOY BATHING

A boy got out of his depth while bathing
in a river and was about to drown.

A man heard his cries for help. He
came to the riverside and began to
scold the boy for being so careless.
"Oh, sir," said the boy, "please save
me first and scold me afterwards."

Give assistance, not advice, in a crisis.

CENTRAL PUBLIC SCHOOL LIBRARY,

THE DOG AND
HIS SHADOW

A dog had found a rather choice bone
and was carrying it home.

Crossing a bridge, he noticed his
reflection in the water.

He thought it was another dog with
an even bigger bone.

He tried to snatch the other dog's bone
but only succeeded in dropping his own.

And so he had no bone at all,
for one was just a reflection
and the other sank out of sight.

*When you grasp at the shadow
you lose the substance.*

THE FOX AND THE CROW

A crow sat on a branch, holding a nice bit of cheese in her beak.

A fox wanted the cheese and had an idea how he might get it.

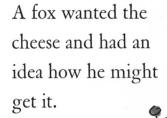

"What a beautiful bird!"
said the fox, loud enough for
the crow to hear. "Surely such
a lovely bird has a lovely voice.
How I long to hear her sing."

19

The foolish bird opened
her mouth to sing. But
all that came out was a
"caw" and the cheese.

The fox ate the cheese
and said, "I see you do
have a voice, Madam Crow.
What you seem to be
lacking is brains."

Don't be fooled by flattery.

21

THE FOX AND THE GRAPES

A hungry fox spied some plump, juicy grapes high on a vine.

He tried and tried to get the grapes,
but they were always just out of reach.

At last the fox was forced to give up.

Hiding his disappointment, he said,
"I didn't want them anyway. Those
grapes are obviously sour."

There's some comfort in pretending
that we don't want what we can't get.

THE GNAT AND
THE BULL

A gnat settled on the horn of a bull
and rested there for quite a long time.

When at last he was ready to leave, the gnat said,
"Will you excuse me? I think I'll go now."

"Go ahead," said the bull. "I didn't notice you when you came, and I won't miss you when you're gone."

Sometimes we seem more important to ourselves than we do to others.

THE GOOSE THAT LAID THE GOLDEN EGGS

A man and his wife had the good fortune
to own a goose that laid golden eggs.

Lucky though they were, they didn't think they were getting rich fast enough, for the goose laid only one egg a day.

Imagining that the goose must be solid
gold inside, they decided to kill her
and get all the treasure at once.
But when they cut her open they found
that she was just like any other goose.

They had roast goose for supper and
that was the end. Wanting more,
they had lost all.

Be content with enough.

THE MILKMAID AND HER PAIL

A milkmaid was carrying a pail of milk on her head and daydreaming about what she would do with it.

"I'll churn this milk into butter," she said. "Then I'll sell the butter and buy some eggs.

"The eggs will hatch and soon I'll have a lot of chickens.

33

"I'll sell some of the
chickens and buy myself
a fine dress. All the
boys will want to dance
with me in my fine
dress. But I'll just say
pooh, pooh! and toss my
head like THIS."

And, forgetting all about the pail,
she tossed her head.

*Don't count your chickens before
they're hatched.*

THE OX AND THE FROG

Some frogs saw an ox.

"How big he is!" said one.

"No bigger than I
could be if I tried,"
said the other,
puffing himself up.
"Am I not now as
big as the ox?"

"Not quite," said his friend.
The boastful frog took
a deeper breath.

"The ox was bigger," said his friend.

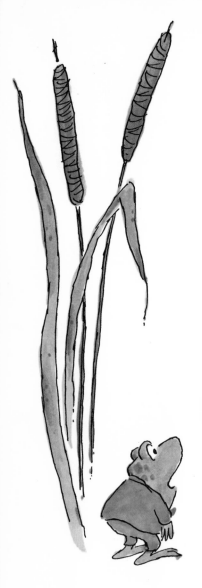

So the boastful frog puffed
and puffed until he got bigger
and bigger.

"The ox was bigger still," said
his friend.

With that the frog took
a very, VERY deep breath...
and burst!

*Every windbag is punctured
sooner or later.*

39

THE SHEPHERD BOY
AND THE WOLF

A shepherd boy thought he would play a joke
on the people in the village nearby. So he cried:

"WOLF! WOLF!"

The people came running to save the sheep.
But of course there wasn't any wolf.

The shepherd boy thought it was
very funny and played the same trick
several times after that.

One day a wolf really did come. The
boy cried, "WOLF! WOLF!" as loud
as he could. But everyone was so used
to hearing him call that they took
no notice.

And the wolf had
his own way with
the sheep.

*You can't believe a liar
even when he tells the truth.*

THE TOWN MOUSE AND THE COUNTRY MOUSE

A Town Mouse went to visit his
country cousin. The Country
Mouse lived very simply.
"Is this all you ever eat?"
asked the Town Mouse.
"In the city I live like
a king! Why don't you come
and live with me?"

44

So when the Town Mouse went back home,
the Country Mouse went along.
Never in his life had the
Country Mouse seen
so many good things
to eat!

But every time they sat down to eat, someone came in and the mice had to run for their lives.

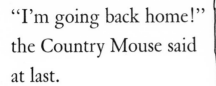

"I'm going back home!"
the Country Mouse said
at last.
"The food may not be
as fancy, but at least
I can eat it in peace."

*A crust in comfort is
better than a feast with fear.*

47

THE WOLF AND THE CRANE

A wolf got a bone stuck in his throat
and promised a crane a reward if she
would pull it out.

The crane put her head into the wolf's
mouth and with her long bill quite
easily removed the bone.

But when she asked for her reward, the wolf just bared his teeth and said:

"You stuck your head into a wolf's
mouth and didn't get it bitten off.
What greater reward could you ask for?"

When you deal with beastly persons
be thankful if you don't lose your head.

THE WOLF IN SHEEP'S CLOTHING

A wolf disguised himself as a sheep
in order to prey upon the flock
undetected.

He mingled with the sheep while they
were at pasture.

His costume completely deceived the
shepherd.

In the evening he was shut up in the fold with the rest.

"I'm going to eat well tonight," said the wolf. But the shepherd returned to get some meat for the next day.

Mistaking the wolf for a sheep, he
killed him on the spot.

*Don't go looking for trouble. You
might find somebody else's.*

JACK KENT is the author of *The Wizard of Wallaby Wallow, The Fat Cat, Mr. Meebles, The Blah, The Grown-up Day* and *Just Only John,* all published by Parents' Magazine Press. He is a free-lance commercial artist and the creator of the comic strip, *King Aroo.* Mr. Kent was born in Burlington, Iowa, and feels that his early years differed from other boys' only in that his family traveled constantly and he received his education at "public and private schools in a long list of cities and states." He was living in San Antonio, Texas, when a local newspaper sent a reporter to interview him in connection with *King Aroo.* He married the reporter, and they are still living happily ever after in San Antonio with their teen-age son, Jack, Jr.